We're going to have a show today!
These instruments can't wait to play.

To start our show we need a band—
maybe *you* can lend a hand!

You can rock on the guitar.
Try it out—you'll be a star!
Give a strum with your thumb:

STRUM, STRUM, STRUM!

Make the drum go RAT-A-TAT!
You can pat it—just like that.
Drum a beat, then repeat:

RAT
-A-
TAT!

RAT
-A-
TAT!

Piano keys lie in a row.
Some play high, and some play low.
Tap these keys, will you please?

tink! tink! tink!

tunk! tunk! tunk!
tunk!

Hey, this band is sounding sweet!
Feel the music in your feet.

ONE, TWO,

Count to four,
then play some more:

"THREE, FOUR..."

Here's some rhythm on a stick!
Maracas rattle: CHICK-CHICK-CHICK.

CHICK-
CHICK-
CHICK-

You can make them—
shake, shake, shake them:

CHICK- CHICK-

CHICK-

CHICK-

CHICK!

A saxophone goes DOO-BEE-DOO.
I can DOO it—you can, too!
Blow that thing,
and make it swing!

The slide trombone is loud and long.
Hold it high, and play it strong.
Slide the slide, on the side:

BWAH!

BWAH!

BWAH—

BWAH-BWAH!

When cymbals clash, they go CRASH!
Close the book, and make them smash.
One, two, three, play with me:

Now you've practiced how to play,
you can play this book *your* way.

STRUM STRUM!

RAT -A- TAT!

tink! tink! tunk! tunk!

CHICK- CHICK- CHICK!

Play along—
we'll make a song:

What a show! Brava! Bravo!
You played this book just like a pro!

Stand up now, and take a bow.

CLAP!
CLAP!
CLAP!

CL

For Kelly with many thanks —J. Y.

For Rob, Spencer, E.J., John, and Kurt —D. W.

First published in the United States of America in May 2018 by Bloomsbury Children's Books
www.bloomsbury.com

Bloomsbury is a registered trademark of Bloomsbury Publishing Plc

For information about permission to reproduce selections from this book, write to
Permissions, Bloomsbury Children's Books, 1385 Broadway, New York, New York 10018
Bloomsbury books may be purchased for business or promotional use. For information on bulk purchases please contact
Macmillan Corporate and Premium Sales Department at specialmarkets@macmillan.com

Library of Congress Cataloging-in-Publication Data
available at https://lccn.loc.gov/2017033366
ISBN 978-1-68119-506-3 (hardcover) • ISBN 978-1-68119-864-4 (e-book) • ISBN 978-1-68119-865-1 (e-PDF)

Art created digitally with Photoshop, custom brushes, and a lot of bright colors
Typeset in Geometric 415 • Book design by Daniel Wiseman and John Candell
Printed in China by Leo Paper Products, Heshan, Guangdong
1 3 5 7 9 10 8 6 4 2

All papers used by Bloomsbury Publishing, Inc., are natural, recyclable products made from wood grown in well-managed forests.
The manufacturing processes conform to the environmental regulations of the country of origin.